SPACE PIRATES

BY DAVID ORME

ILLUSTRATED BY
PAUL SAVAGE

Librarian Reviewer
Joanne Bongaarts
Educational Consultant
MS in Library Media Education, Minnesota State University, Mankato, MN
Teacher and Media Specialist with Edina Public Schools, MN, 1993–2000

Reading Consultant
Elizabeth Stedem
Educator/Consultant, Colorado Springs, CO
MA in Elementary Education, University of Denver, CO

▼▼ STONE ARCH BOOKS
Minneapolis   San Diego

First published in the United States in 2006
by Stone Arch Books,
151 Good Counsel Drive, P.O. Box 669,
Mankato, Minnesota 56002.
www.stonearchbooks.com

Originally published in Great Britain in 2004
by Badger Publishing Ltd.

Library of Congress Cataloging-in-Publication Data
Orme, David.
    Space Pirates / by David Orme; illustrated by Paul Savage.
    p. cm. — Keystone Books.
    Summary: The crew of the *Nightstar* is on a cargo mission in deep
space when their ship is attacked by space pirates.
    ISBN-13: 978-1-59889-016-7 (library binding)
    ISBN-10: 1-59889-016-6 (hardcover)
    ISBN-13: 978-1-59889-187-4 (library binding)
    ISBN-10: 1-59889-187-1 (paperback)
    [1. Pirates—Fiction. 2. Science fiction.] I. Savage, Paul, 1971– ill.
II. Title.
PZ7.O6338Spa 2006
[Fic]—dc22   2005026144

1 2 3 4 5 6 11 10 09 08 07 06

TABLE OF CONTENTS

Chapter 1

A Big Problem

"Engineering! Report, please! Todd, what's going on?" Captain Street needed to know.

It had been quiet on the bridge of the *Nightstar*. The cargo ship almost flew itself on long journeys between the stars. There wasn't much for the captain and crew to do.

Until now.

The ship gave a sudden shudder. Then the red warning lights started to flash. Captain Street quickly checked the control panel, but she could not tell what was wrong.

Todd reported back from the engine room. "I don't understand it. The warp engine cut out, and then it started again. It's never done that before."

"What do you think we should do?" asked the captain.

"I'd like to shut down the engine and check it out. It shouldn't take long," Todd replied.

"Okay. Report back when it's done," the captain ordered.

The crew on the bridge listened for the deep hum of the warp engine to die away, but nothing changed.

At last, Todd spoke again. "Captain, we've got a problem. I can't shut down the engine's computer. It's locked me out. It's running a program. Something has taken over the computer!"

Just then Tess broke in. She was in charge of the ship's radio. "There's a powerful radio signal coming in. It's sending computer code!"

There was only one explanation. Their ship was being attacked! They had to do something quickly.

"Todd, knock out the fuses on the main power supply," ordered Captain Street.

This was a dangerous thing to do. The crew's life-support system needed the power, but they had to get control of the ship.

"Knocking out fuses, now," Todd reported to the captain.

There was a terrible yell from the engine room.

"Todd, what happened? Are you okay?" asked the captain.

It took a long time for Todd to reply. "I'm okay, Captain. But I got a huge shock from the power supply. Whatever it is, it doesn't want me to shut down the computer."

"Captain, look at this!" Baz yelled.

Baz, the ship's navigator, was staring at a computer screen in alarm.

"There's another ship out there. That must be where the radio signal is coming from. And that's not all. It's making us change course, and there's nothing I can do about it."

"What's the new course?" the captain asked.

Baz checked and checked again. "It's bad news. We're heading straight for the Ghost Nebula!"

Chapter 2

INTO THE NEBULA

Nebulas were one of the many dangers in outer space. They were huge clouds of gases and stars. The dust and gas particles were spread very thinly. But because spaceships traveled so fast, even small particles could cause great damage. Worse, the gases were charged with electricity. This stopped a ship's computers from working.

"How long until we reach the edge of the nebula?" asked Captain Street.

"About two hours," replied Baz.

The Ghost Nebula stretched across the view-screen. White arms of glowing gases reached out toward them like a poisonous spider. Inside the nebula, misty-looking stars shined colorfully.

"Look there," Baz said suddenly. "There's a way into the nebula that's clear of gases. That's where we're being taken."

An hour later, they entered the dark pathway through the nebula. On and on they went, following the mysterious spaceship that had captured them. At last they saw a bright star.

"That star has planets," said Baz. "That must be where we're going."

Then two things happened. First, the ship started to slow down.

Second, they heard the sound of air being pumped out into space.

"Someone's trying to kill us!" shouted Captain Street. "Spacesuits on. Then down to the cargo bay, quickly!"

"What's the plan?" Baz asked.

"There's no time to explain! Just do it!" the captain ordered.

The *Nightstar's* crew was lucky. The cargo included equipment to set up a new space station in orbit around a planet. One piece of cargo was a lander used to travel between a space station and a planet. The lander had its own life-support system.

By the time they got to the cargo bay, there was no air left in the ship.

Their suits would only give them air for a couple of hours. Without the lander, they could not survive.

Todd opened the air lock. Outside, the great nebula was glowing.

"Inside the lander, quick!" the captain ordered.

Captain Street took the controls. Carefully, she guided the lander out of the air-lock door.

"Where are we heading, Captain?" asked Todd.

"We have no other choice," said the captain. "It's that planet or death!"

Chapter 3

SPACE PIRATES

Baz checked the surface of the planet through the long-distance viewer.

"Look at that!" he exclaimed.

They all looked at the screen. The planet had blue seas and deep-green forests like Earth. Baz had figured out the direction of the *Nightstar* and saw something else.

"Near that mountain range is a spaceport," said Baz. "There must be a dozen spaceships. What's going on?"

Captain Street looked grimly at the screen. "Space pirates! Ships have been missing lately — too many. No one would ever think of looking for pirates in a nebula. That radio-control trick is clever, too. I think I can guess who's behind this."

"So can I," said Todd. "It must be Dr. Drake!"

Dr. Drake had once been a great scientist. Now he was a powerful criminal. Four years ago he was sent to the space prison on Mars. Two years ago he escaped. No one had seen him since.

They watched as the *Nightstar* was carefully guided down onto the spaceport.

"They'll get a big surprise when they find out there's no crew!" grinned Todd.

"They'll see the open cargo door," explained the captain. "They may think we were sucked out into space. We'll wait here until night."

"Then we can land in the forest about five miles from the base," the captain continued. "We'll walk from there. It's important that they don't know we're on the planet."

"Do you have a plan, Captain?" Todd asked.

"No, but I'm open to ideas!" the captain replied.

* * *

It was a long, hard walk. The alien forest was dark and threatening. In the distance, they could hear the sound of huge beasts roaring and the cries of their victims.

The spacesuits were difficult to walk in, but at least they made sure that insects couldn't bite the crew. The planet's air was safe to breathe, but the helmets had special filters to remove any dangerous viruses.

At last the crew saw bright lights ahead of them. They had reached the edge of the spaceport.

Chapter 4

THE SLEEPY GUARD

The pirates had set up bright lights around the spaceport. Spaceships they had captured stood quiet and empty. Near one side was the pirates' own ship. Its air lock was open.

"The *Nightstar* is over there," the captain whispered. "Look! They're unloading the cargo now."

Four men were heading into the air lock.

At that moment, Captain Street knew what they had to do. "Head for the pirate ship!"

They ran around the side of the spaceport, trying to avoid the lights in case they were seen. After several minutes they reached the air lock of the pirate ship.

"Todd, stay out here and keep watch," the captain ordered. "We'll go in and see what's going on."

They crept up to the bridge. A man was sitting back in a chair, feet up on the control desk. He seemed to be napping. It wasn't Drake. Captain Street guessed the doctor himself must be on the *Nightstar.*

Baz crept forward and grabbed the pirate around the neck. The pirate almost fell out of his chair with shock. He reached down for a weapon, but Captain Street got there first, kicking it away from him.

In one corner there was a pile of supplies. Tess found a coil of thick wire. "Use this to tie him up."

But the pirate didn't want to be tied up. He kicked and yelled, even when Captain Street threatened him with his own gun. They all held him down together and managed to tie him up.

They were so busy holding the pirate down that they didn't notice a door slowly opening on the other side of the bridge.

"That's enough!" A tall, gray-haired man stood in the doorway. It was Dr. Drake.

Chapter 5

DR. DRAKE IN CONTROL

The doctor was carrying a weapon. There was nothing the crew could do. They moved away from the man they had tied up. He seemed more scared of Dr. Drake than they were. He had let the doctor down.

Dr. Drake spoke into a radio. "Have you cleared the ship, yet? Good. Stay where you are for the moment. We have visitors."

"I'm going to send them on a little ride," added the doctor.

He suddenly noticed that Baz was looking carefully at the control panel. "You! Come away from there! Outside, all of you!" commanded the doctor.

"What about me?" asked the other pirate. He was still tied up. "Aren't you going to untie me?"

"No! You can stay like that as a punishment for being useless!" Then Drake turned to the *Nightstar's* crew. "Now move, and don't try anything!"

Captain Street, Baz, and Tess did as they were told. The weapon Dr. Drake held looked deadly.

Dr. Drake marched them out of the spaceship and across the spaceport to the *Nightstar*.

"I'm going to send you on an interesting journey," Dr. Drake explained. "No one has ever gone into the center of a nebula. That's where you're going!"

Captain Street was angry with herself. She was in charge, and she had let her crew down. "Why don't you just kill us now and be done with it?"

"Much too messy, Captain," Dr. Drake replied. "Now get on board."

But there was a problem. When they reached the *Nightstar*, the air-lock door was locked shut.

It was Dr. Drake's turn to be angry. He spoke into his radio. "What's going on? Open the air lock, you fools!"

Slowly, the air-lock door swung open. There stood Todd with a pirate's gun in each hand.

Chapter 6

DOCTOR TAKES A RIDE

"You didn't expect me, did you, Doctor?" Todd yelled. "Don't worry, Captain. I haven't joined the pirates!"

Dr. Drake stepped back in surprise. Tess took her chance. With a high kick, she knocked the weapon out of the doctor's hand.

Todd had heard Baz, Tess, and the captain coming out of the pirate ship.

Todd managed to slip across to the
Nightstar before they got there.

"You need to feed your men better,
Dr. Drake," Todd explained. "I found
them having a meal from our ship's
supplies. They had put their weapons
down, ready for me to find!"

"Where are they now?" asked Captain Street.

"I locked them in the storeroom," Todd replied. "They don't seem to like it in there!"

Banging and shouting could be heard coming from the storeroom.

"Well done, Todd!" the captain exclaimed. "I think Dr. Drake better join them. He might be able to keep them quiet!"

Captain Street turned to the doctor. "I think it's your turn to take a ride, Doctor, but I think you'll find it's a lot more boring than the one you promised me!"

* * *

Baz soon figured out how the
pirates' radio-control system worked. A
few hours later, the pirate ship took off
with Captain Street at the controls.

The *Nightstar*, with the pirates still on board, took off, too. Baz controlled it from the bridge of the pirate ship. The *Nightstar* followed them out of the nebula and on a course to Earth.

Captain Street spoke to the pirates on the ship's radio. "It's going to take a week to get back to Earth, so I hope you manage to get out of the storeroom. If not, you're going to get hungry. But don't worry. I'm sure there'll be a good meal waiting for you when you arrive at the space prison!"

ABOUT THE AUTHOR

David Orme taught school for 18 years before becoming a full-time writer. He has written over 200 books about tornadoes, orangutans, soccer, space travel, and other topics.

In his free time, David enjoys taking his granddaughter, Sarah, on adventures, climbing nearby mountains and visiting London graveyards. He lives in Hampshire, England, with his wife, Helen, who is also a writer.

ABOUT THE ILLUSTRATOR

Paul Savage works in a design studio. He says illustrating books is "the best job." He's always been interested in illustrating books, and he loves reading. Paul also enjoys playing sports and running.

He lives in England with his wife and daughter, Amelia.

GLOSSARY

bridge (BRIJ)—the place inside a ship where the crew controls the ship

cargo (KAR-goh)—items that are carried by a ship; a cargo ship carries cargo from place to place.

fuse (FYOOZ)—a safety device in electrical equipment that cuts off the power when something goes wrong

lander (LAND-ur)—a small spacecraft used to travel between a planet and a larger ship

navigator (NAV-uh-gate-ur)—the person in charge of guiding a ship as it travels

nebula (NEB-yoo-luh)—a bright, cloudlike mass of stars, gases, and dust particles

orbit (OR-bit)—the invisible path followed by an object circling a planet or sun

port (PORT)—a place where ships can safely land

virus (VYE-ruhss)—a very tiny organism that causes disease

DISCUSSION QUESTIONS

1. After Doctor Drake captures the crew inside the pirate ship, Captain Street becomes angry with herself. Why do you think she feels this way?

2. Captain Street told Todd to stay outside and stand guard while the rest of the crew went inside the pirate ship. But Todd snuck back into the *Nightstar*. Was it okay for him to disobey the captain's orders?

3. Both Captain Street and Doctor Drake are in charge of crews. How do they treat their crew members? Which crew would you want to join and why?

WRITING
PROMPTS

1. Write about how this story would be different if it took place on a boat in the ocean instead of on a ship in space. Did the *Nightstar's* crew face special challenges in outer space? What challenges might they face at sea?

2. Write about what you might find if you landed on an alien planet. What does the planet look like? Are there other life forms on the planet?

3. Imagine that you are the captain of the *Nightstar*. Write about what you would do if space pirates captured you and your crew. How would you escape?

ALSO BY
DAVID ORME

Something Evil

A big city is built on the shore of Dark Lake, which can only mean one thing — big trouble. Discover who, or what, is causing the people living near Dark Lake to disappear.

Space Wreck

Space explorers Sam and Simon are traveling in search of space crystals when their ship suddenly loses power and crashes on an asteroid. Will Sam and Simon find a way to get off the asteroid?

OTHER BOOKS IN THIS SET

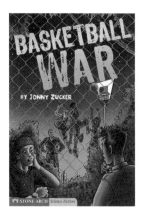

Basketball War
by Jonny Zucker

Jim and Ali are determined to beat the Langham Jets in the upcoming basketball championship. But the boys learn that there's something strange about their rival's new coach.

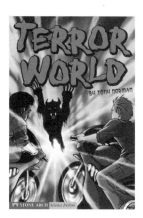

Terror World
by Tony Norman

Jimmy and Seb love playing the games at Terror World arcade. When the owner offers them a free trial of a new game, they enter the real "Terror World." Chased by razor cats, it seems they have no escape.

INTERNET SITES

Do you want to know more about subjects related to this book? Or are you interested in learning about other topics? Then check out FactHound, a fun, easy way to find Internet sites.

Our investigative staff has already sniffed out great sites for you!

Here's how to use FactHound:

1. Visit *www.facthound.com*

2. Select your grade level.

3. To learn more about subjects related to this book, type in the book's ISBN number: **1598890166**.

4. Click the **Fetch It** button.

FactHound will fetch the best Internet sites for you!